BRATZ™ vs. BOYZ™

Grosset & Dunlap • New York

www.bratzpack.com

TM & © 2004 MGA Entertainment, Inc. Bratz and all related logos, names and distinctive likenesses are the exclusive property of MGA Entertainment, Inc. All Rights Reserved.

Used under license by Penguin Young Readers Group. Published by Grosset & Dunlap, a division of Penguin Young Readers Group, 345 Hudson Street, New York, New York 10014. GROSSET & DUNLAP is a trademark of Penguin Group (USA) Inc. Printed in the U.S.A.

Library of Congress Cataloging-in-Publication Data

Bratz vs. Boyz.
   p. cm. — (Bratz Boyz)
  Summary: The Bratz and the Boyz compete to create moneymaking projects that will benefit their community.
  ISBN 0-448-43624-8 (pbk.)
  [1. Moneymaking projects—Fiction. 2. Voluntarism—Fiction. 3. Schools—Fiction.] I. Title: Bratz versus Boyz. II. Bratz Boyz (Series)
  PZ7.B6973 2004
  [E]—dc22

ISBN 0-448-43624-8   10 9 8 7 6 5 4 3 2 1

Hello, I'm **Sasha**™! My friends call me "Bunny Boo" because I'm way into the hip-hop thang! I also love urban street wear like rockin' denim skirts and fresh hats. As you can probably guess, I love dance parties—especially with my girls!

Hey! **Jade**™ here. Sometimes I go by "Kool Kat" because I love Xtreme kool styles. I'm always the first to try out far-out fashion and I love to scout out new trends before anyone else does. In fashion, and also in life—I like to be daring!

Hey there! I'm **Cloe™**! My friends call me "Angel" 'cause that's what I am. My girls and I share everything—from super slumber parties to relaxing spa treatments to major shopping sprees. Above all, we share a passion for fashion! But while we all love to try out new styles, we each definitely have our own special taste. I love to wear sparkly, shimmery fabrics—things that make me feel like a star in the sky!

Hi! **Yasmin™** here! People call me "Princess" because I rule with a cool head. I love to wear clothes in earthy colors and textures—maybe because I'm so down-to-earth! And when I'm not out with my girls hittin' the shops, you can find me buried in a great book—or writing something of my own! I love to Xpress myself in my journal.

Yo! It's **Koby™** comin' at ya! My boys and I love hangin' with our friends the Bratz, and we crave Xtreme adventure! My friends call me "The Panther" 'cause I'm always on the prowl. I love sports—but my favorite is surfin'! I also love to make movies. I have an awesome video cam that I use all the time.

Eitan™ here. I go by "The Dragon" because I'm a nonstop hotshot. I love to kick back with my crew, and when I'm on my own, I'm way into comics, video games, and electronics.

I'm **Dylan™**. You can call me "The Fox" because I'm so slick. Like Bunny Boo, I love hip-hop music and slammin' urban style. Dance parties and deejaying are totally my thang!

W'sup! **Cameron™** here! I'm into boardin', big-time! My boys call me "The Blaze" because I'm on fire. When I'm not chillin' with my buddies, you can find me trickin' out on my skateboard, practicing some new moves.

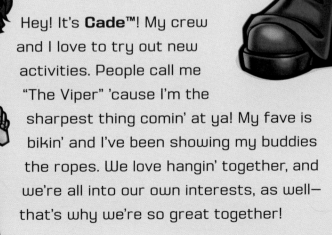

Hey! It's **Cade™**! My crew and I love to try out new activities. People call me "The Viper" 'cause I'm the sharpest thing comin' at ya! My fave is bikin' and I've been showing my buddies the ropes. We love hangin' together, and we're all into our own interests, as well—that's why we're so great together!

My girls and I love shopping, but we love school, too. Okay, so pop quizzes are no fun, but our teacher is way cool.

Yeah, he's always thinking of new projects for us and ways to keep class interesting. Most of the projects we do are cool enough that we hardly even notice we're learning. No kidding!

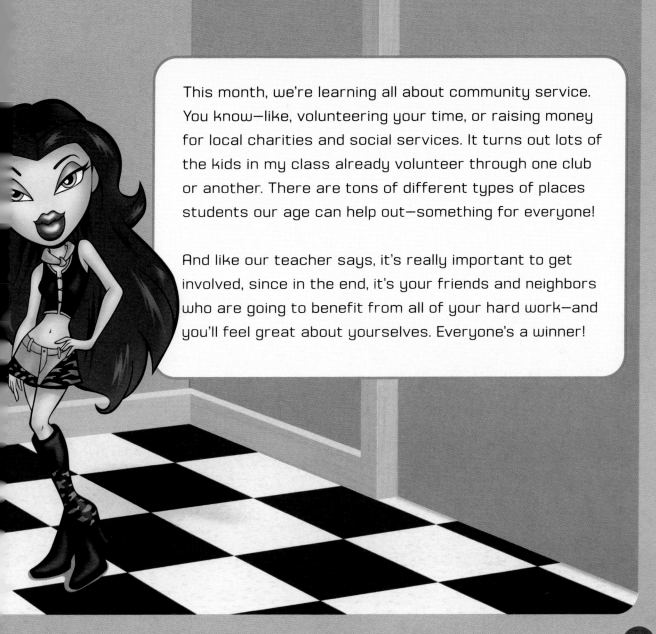

This month, we're learning all about community service. You know—like, volunteering your time, or raising money for local charities and social services. It turns out lots of the kids in my class already volunteer through one club or another. There are tons of different types of places students our age can help out—something for everyone!

And like our teacher says, it's really important to get involved, since in the end, it's your friends and neighbors who are going to benefit from all of your hard work—and you'll feel great about yourselves. Everyone's a winner!

Today our teacher announced that he's assigning us a new project to help us learn about community service. We're going to have a community service drive. The class is going to split up into groups and come up with ways to raise money for our favorite causes.

And the coolest part about it (other than raising money for charity, that is)? The group whose project raises the most money wins a free pizza party at our favorite local pizza parlor! Awesome!

The class split up into groups. Of course, my girls and I wanted to work together, and our teacher agreed—he knows we're a fab team. I suggested that we have a canned food drive. We could collect canned food and donate it to the local food kitchen. Everyone thought it was a great idea.

Almost *too* great, we learned. Another group beat us to it!

Yasmin thought it'd be fun to have a bake sale and donate the profits to our neighborhood parks and playgrounds . . . but then Jade reminded her of what happened the last time she baked. The brownies she made for our last sleepover would have been delicious—if she had remembered to take them out of the oven before they burned!

We just didn't know what to do . . . That's when inspiration hit! Jade had just taken a class in beading, and she was getting really good at making cool jewelry. Her accessories were rockin'! Lots of kids in our class had already asked her to make things for them. So I thought—why not? Jade could teach us how to bead, and we could sell our creations to our classmates, our friends, and all around the neighborhood. Best of all, we could donate the proceeds to the local youth center, the place where neighborhood kids come to chill while their parents are working. Everyone loved my suggestion—especially our teacher!

My boys and I were totally psyched to hear about the community service project. We knew it would be fun to work together and we liked the idea that we'd be helping people, too. Since I love to play with animals, I thought the answer was obvious—we could dog-walk for charity and donate the money to an animal shelter! Everyone thought it was a good idea, but there was one problem—we didn't know anyone who needed new dog-walkers! So we had to forget about that plan.

Dogs would have been fun, no doubt, but you've gotta go where the jobs are! So Koby had another idea. He thought it'd be cool to donate all of our used sports equipment to the youth center in town. I mean, we've got lots of gear that we don't use every day and Koby knew there are some kids out there who could really use it! But Dylan reminded us that some of his best equipment had been gifts from his parents, so he wasn't crazy about giving it away— which we could totally understand. So it was back to the drawing board.

We were out of ideas, when suddenly, Eitan realized—we're all big into cars, so why not spend the day with them? That's right—a car wash! We would definitely raise some serious cash by spending a day sudsing cars down. But where would we donate our funds?

We realized that in school, we had plenty of great sports equipment in gym class and art supplies in art class, and lots and lots of library books, but some schools aren't so lucky. So we decided to donate our money to a nearby school in need. Our teacher thought it was a great idea.

We were really proud of ourselves for coming up with such a cool idea—we could become hot accessory designers and raise money for charity at the same time. But that afternoon at the local pizza parlor, we overheard the boys talking about their car wash.

We all knew the boys would do a great job, but we couldn't help but tease them anyway—just for fun. We reminded them that girls *rule*—and that we'd be the ones to raise the most money!

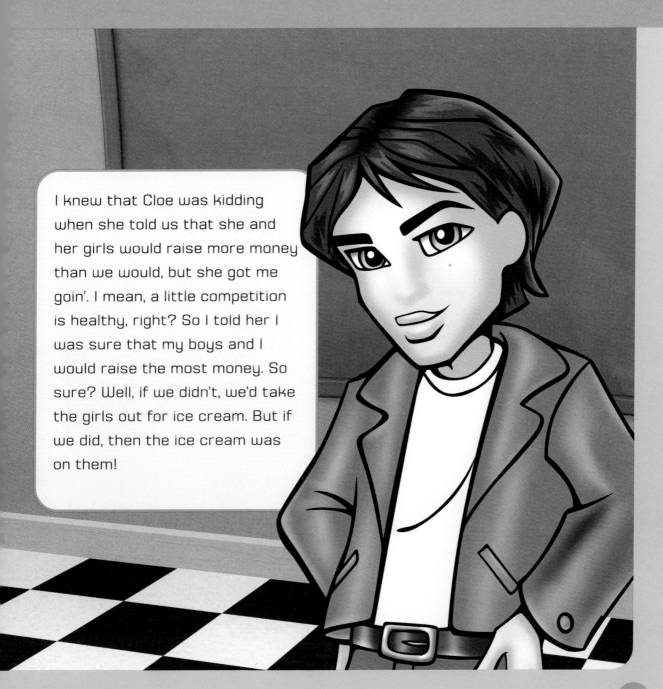

I knew that Cloe was kidding when she told us that she and her girls would raise more money than we would, but she got me goin'. I mean, a little competition is healthy, right? So I told her I was sure that my boys and I would raise the most money. So sure? Well, if we didn't, we'd take the girls out for ice cream. But if we did, then the ice cream was on them!

MY GIRLS AND I EAGERLY ACCEPTED CADE'S CHALLENGE! I TOLD ALL OF MY FRIENDS THAT, AS THE WRITER OF THE GROUP, I WANTED TO KEEP A JOURNAL OF THE WORK THAT WENT INTO OUR JEWELRY DESIGNING. EVERYONE WAS PSYCHED TO KNOW THAT WE'D HAVE A RECORD OF ALL OF OUR HARD WORK EVEN AFTER THE PROJECT WAS OVER AND—WITH ANY LUCK—ALL OF THE JEWELRY WAS SOLD.

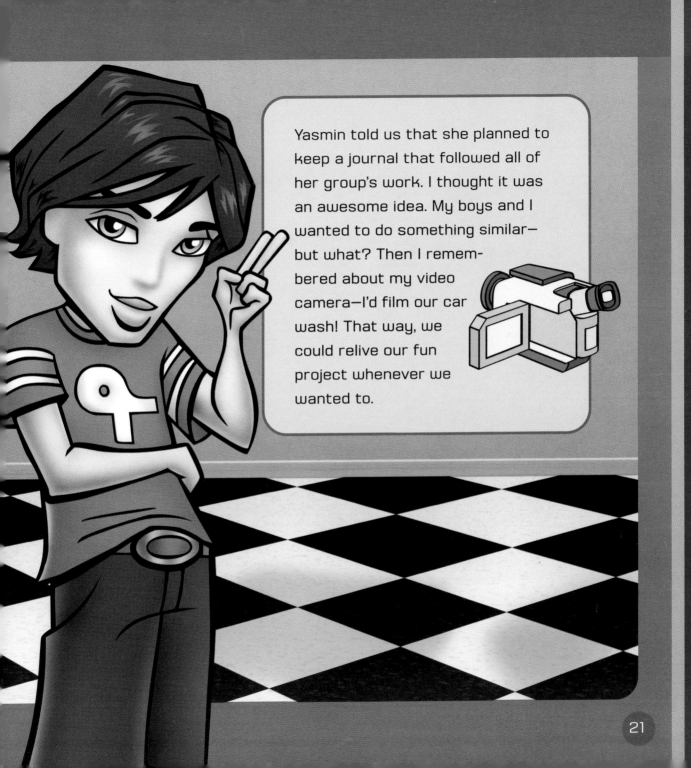

Yasmin told us that she planned to keep a journal that followed all of her group's work. I thought it was an awesome idea. My boys and I wanted to do something similar—but what? Then I remembered about my video camera—I'd film our car wash! That way, we could relive our fun project whenever we wanted to.

Making jewelry wasn't exactly what we expected!
Coming up with superstylin' designs was easy, but stringing beads on teeny tiny wires and hooks was not! Finally, we got the hang of it, though, and our passion for fashion totally paid off. I made a cool cuff bracelet with denim fabric, and Cloe made some barrettes by gluing gorgeous, glittery ribbon to regular plastic barrettes. Jade strung some bright beads together to make Xtreme dangling earrings, and Yasmin used thick leather cord to make a choker necklace. And that was just the beginning!

ur car wash was as much fun as we expected. First, we had to buy supplies, like soap, buckets, and sponges. Our parents gave us old rags that we could use for lathering, wiping, and waxing. We advertised our car wash all around town and held it in Dylan's driveway. We were ready!

Of course, we like to look cool no matter what we're doing, and we learned the hard way that running a car wash was no time to try out new clothing styles—not after Eitan got drenched with a runaway hose! We all laughed as he stood there, dripping wet, but Dylan stepped up with a dry pair of pants and a T-shirt. Lesson learned!

JEWELRY
and
HAIR
ACCESSORIES

FUNKADELIK DESIGNS
FROM STUDENTS LIKE YOU

ON SALE NOW
FOR CHARITY

VISIT OUR STAND OUTSIDE
THE SCHOOL LIBRARY

CHARITY CAR WASH

TODAY AT 3PM

HAVE YOUR CAR WASHED BY THE NEWEST PROS ON THE BLOCK

SUPPORT OUR SCHOOL SYSTEM

CALL DYLAN

Monday morning, our classmates were in bright and early. Everyone was seriously psyched to report the results of their charity. It sounded like everyone's projects had been a major success, and we had raised a ton of money for community programs.

Our teacher was thrilled to hear about what a great job we had all done. And he loved the fact that Yasmin had kept a journal of the experience and that Koby had made a movie. He thought it was a great way to document the project—something we could use for ourselves and show to other classes, too.

I read a passage from my journal to the class that afternoon.

BUNNY BOO, KOOL KAT, ANGEL, AND I HAD A HARD TIME COMING UP WITH THE RIGHT PROJECT FOR THIS ASSIGNMENT. BUT WORKING TOGETHER, WE REALIZED THAT MAKING JEWELRY WAS PERFECT FOR US—IT GAVE US A CHANCE TO DO GOOD WHILE DOING SOMETHING THAT WE LOVE—DESIGNING XTREME FASHIONS! NOT ONLY DID WE RAISE THE MONEY THAT WE WERE SUPPOSED TO, BUT WE LEARNED SOMETHING NEW, AND HAD FUN DOING IT! EVEN IF WE HAVEN'T RAISED THE MOST MONEY, I'D SAY MY GIRLS AND I ARE DEFINITE WINNERS!

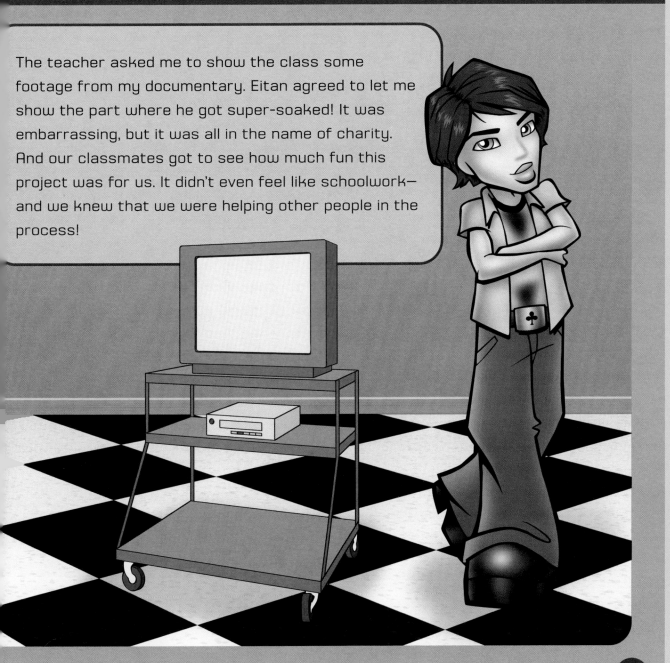

The teacher asked me to show the class some footage from my documentary. Eitan agreed to let me show the part where he got super-soaked! It was embarrassing, but it was all in the name of charity. And our classmates got to see how much fun this project was for us. It didn't even feel like schoolwork— and we knew that we were helping other people in the process!

The class loved our movie, and I was sure my boys and I had raised the most cash. But I was in for a surprise—the girls and the boys were *tied*! The class agreed that the youth center would get half of all the money that we raised, and the other half would go to new school supplies for other students.

...was nice to know that some of the money was ...ng to a school that needed it! We could buy ...w books, new gym supplies, new paints for the ... room—that other students could enjoy! And ... kids at the youth center would get new ...mes, toys, and books, too!

This project rocked and we learned a lot. Girls and boys can *both* rule! Sharing rules, too, and so does friendship. We invited the whole class to our joint pizza party, and afterward, we *all* went out for ice cream—together!